Tim's Din

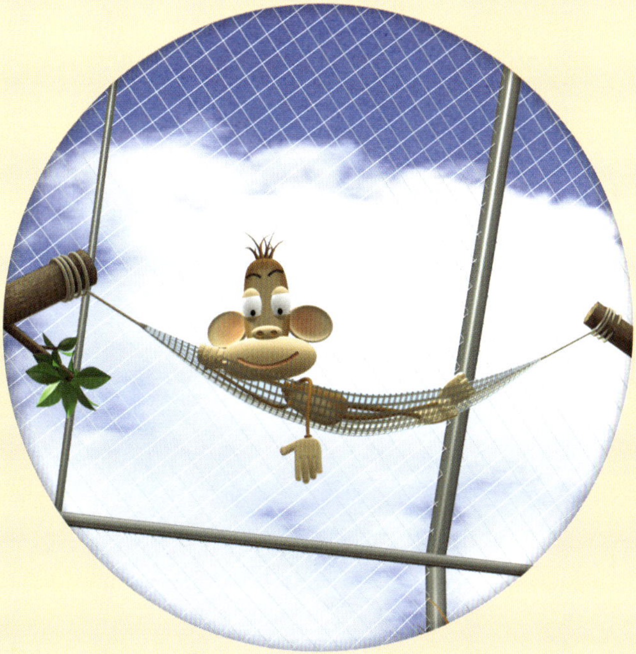

Written by Monica Hughes
Illustrated by Bill Ledger

AF010597

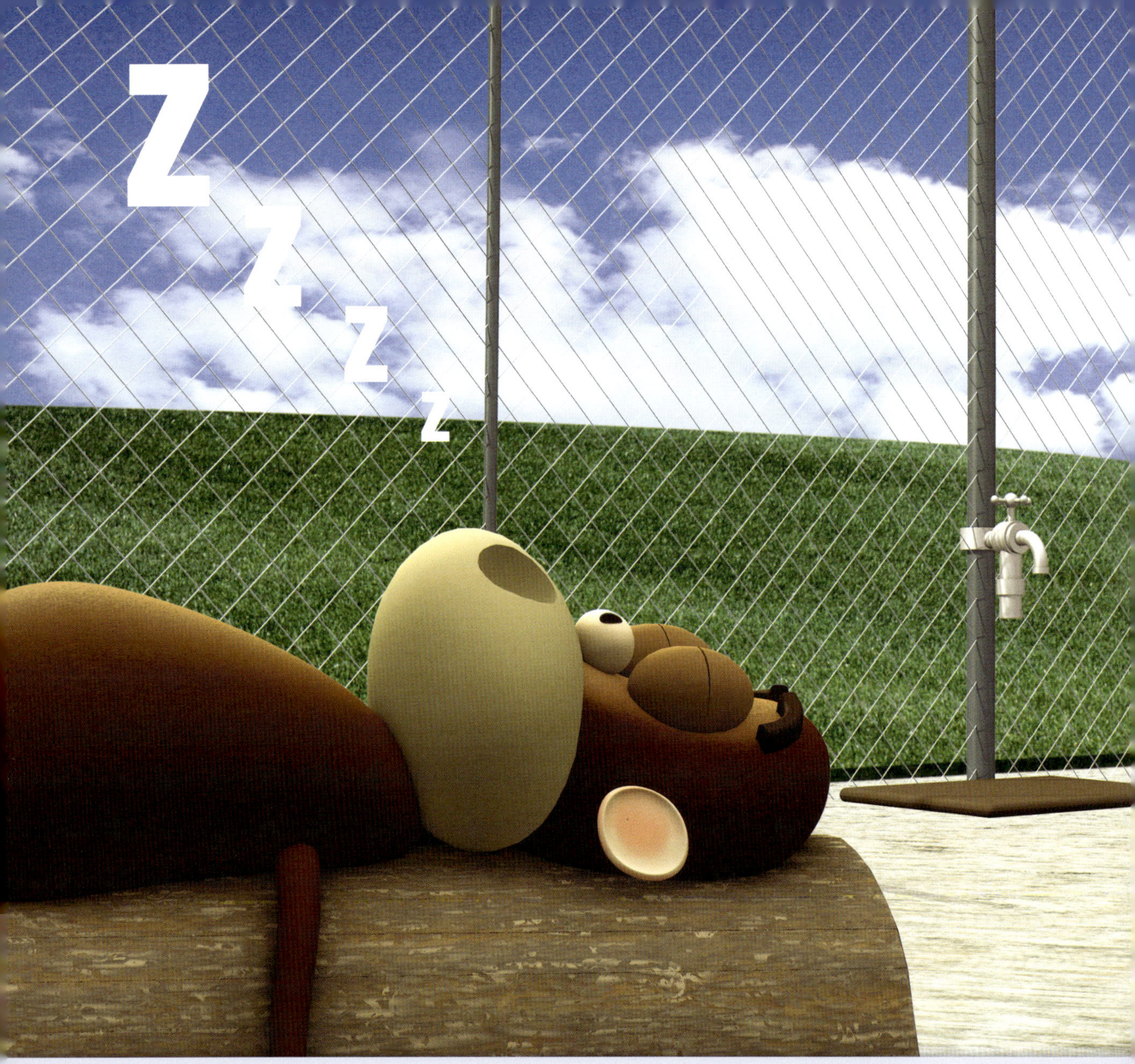

Dad naps.

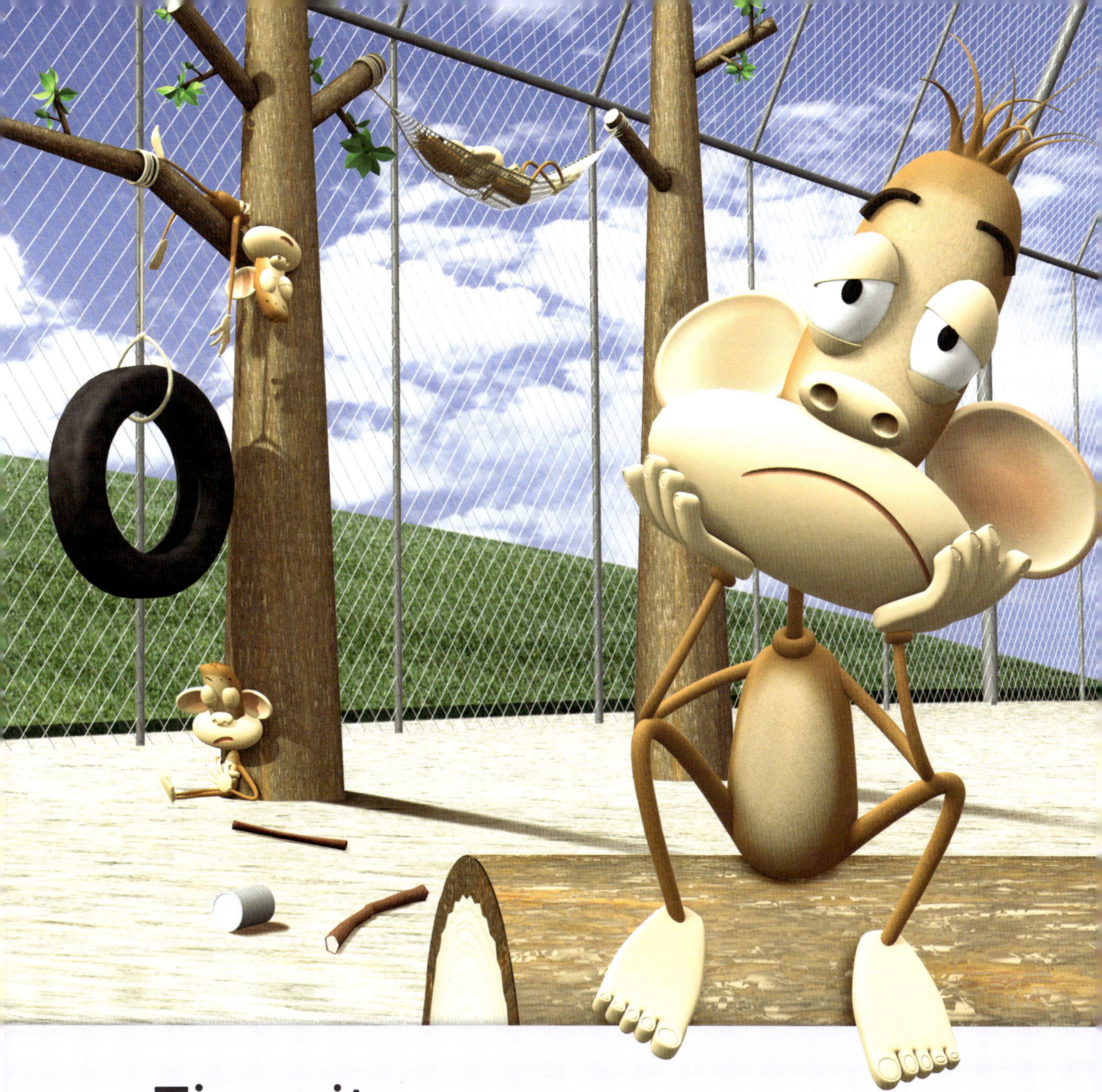

Tim sits.

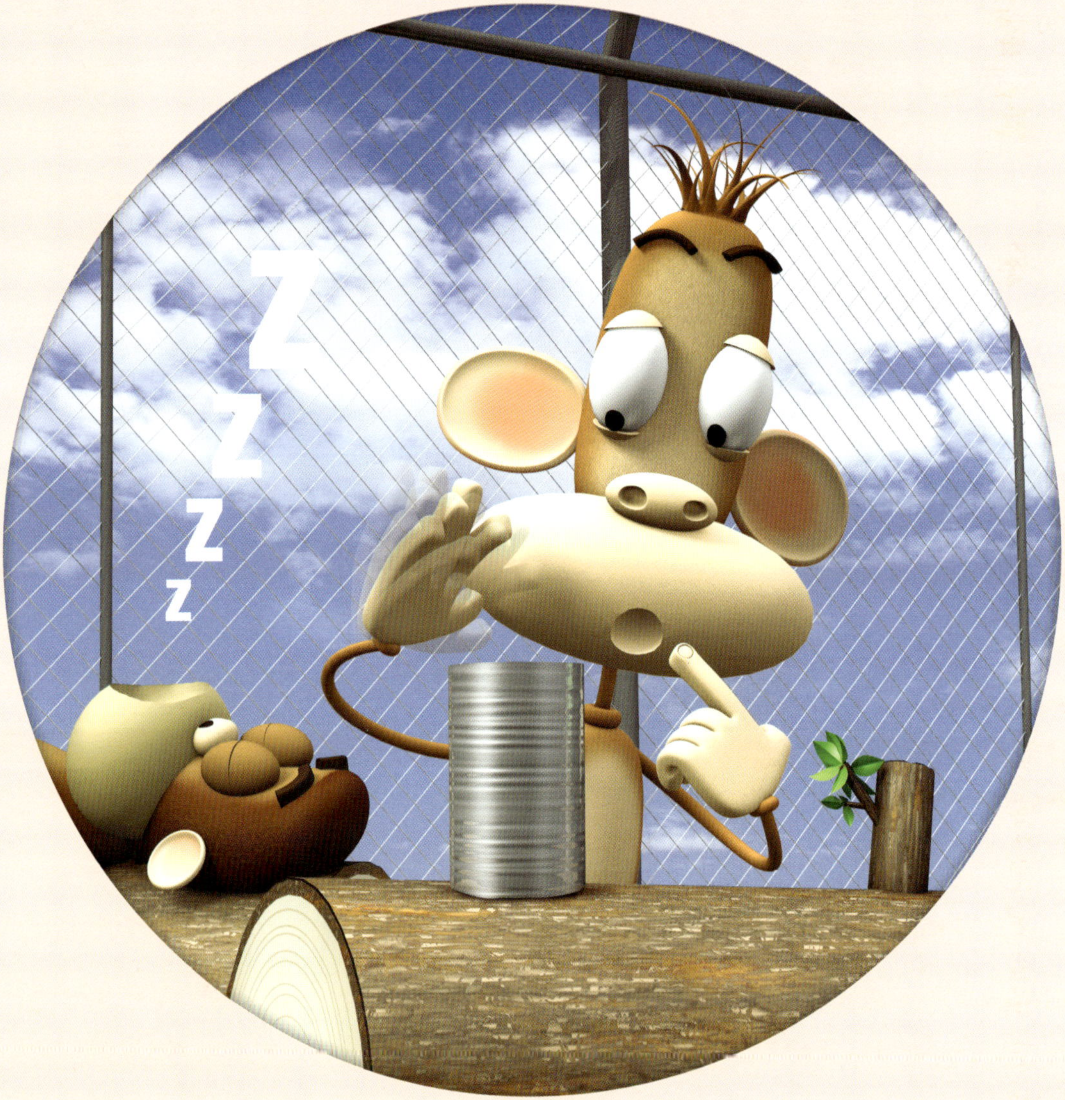

Tim pats a tin.

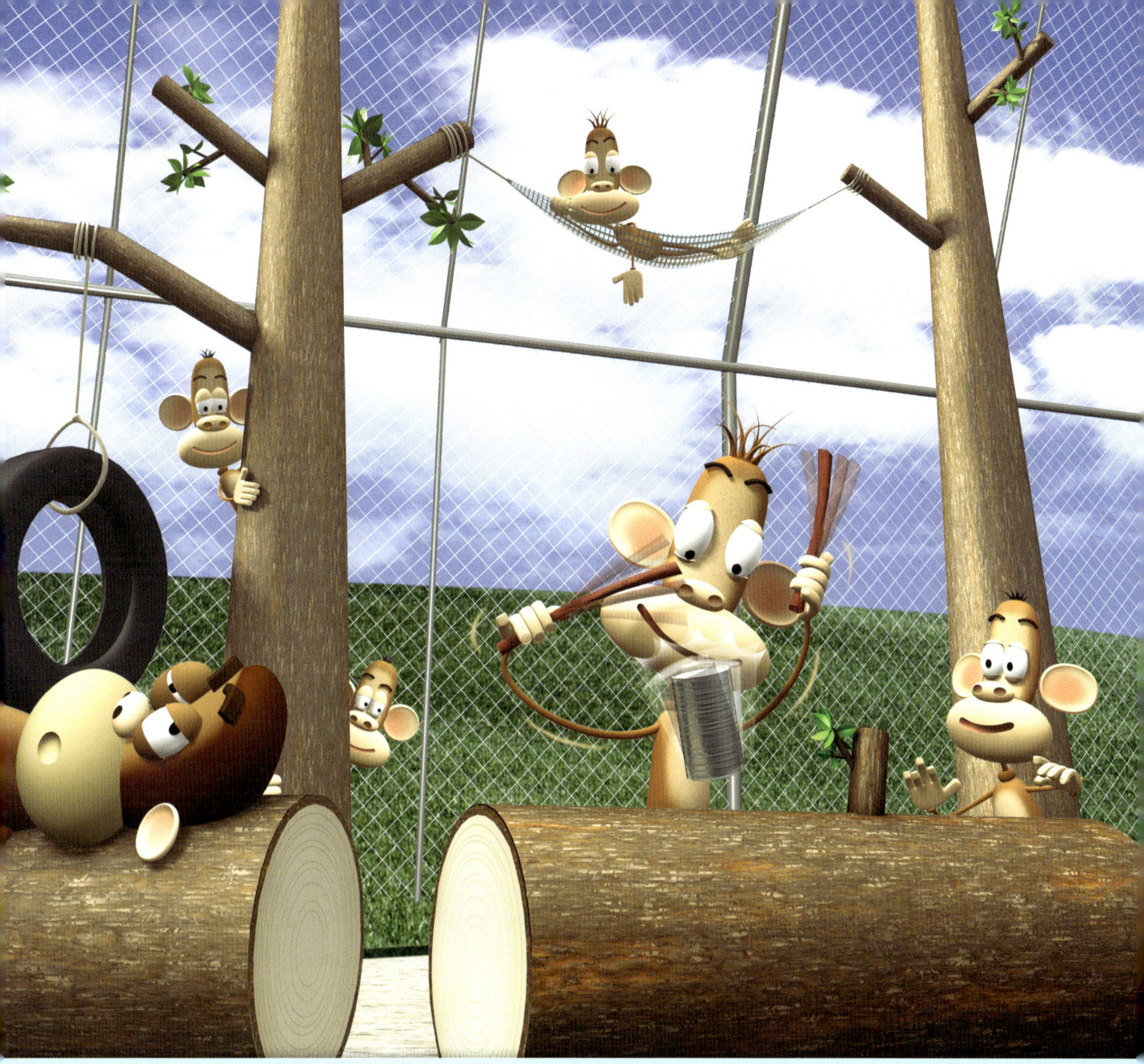

Tim taps a tin.

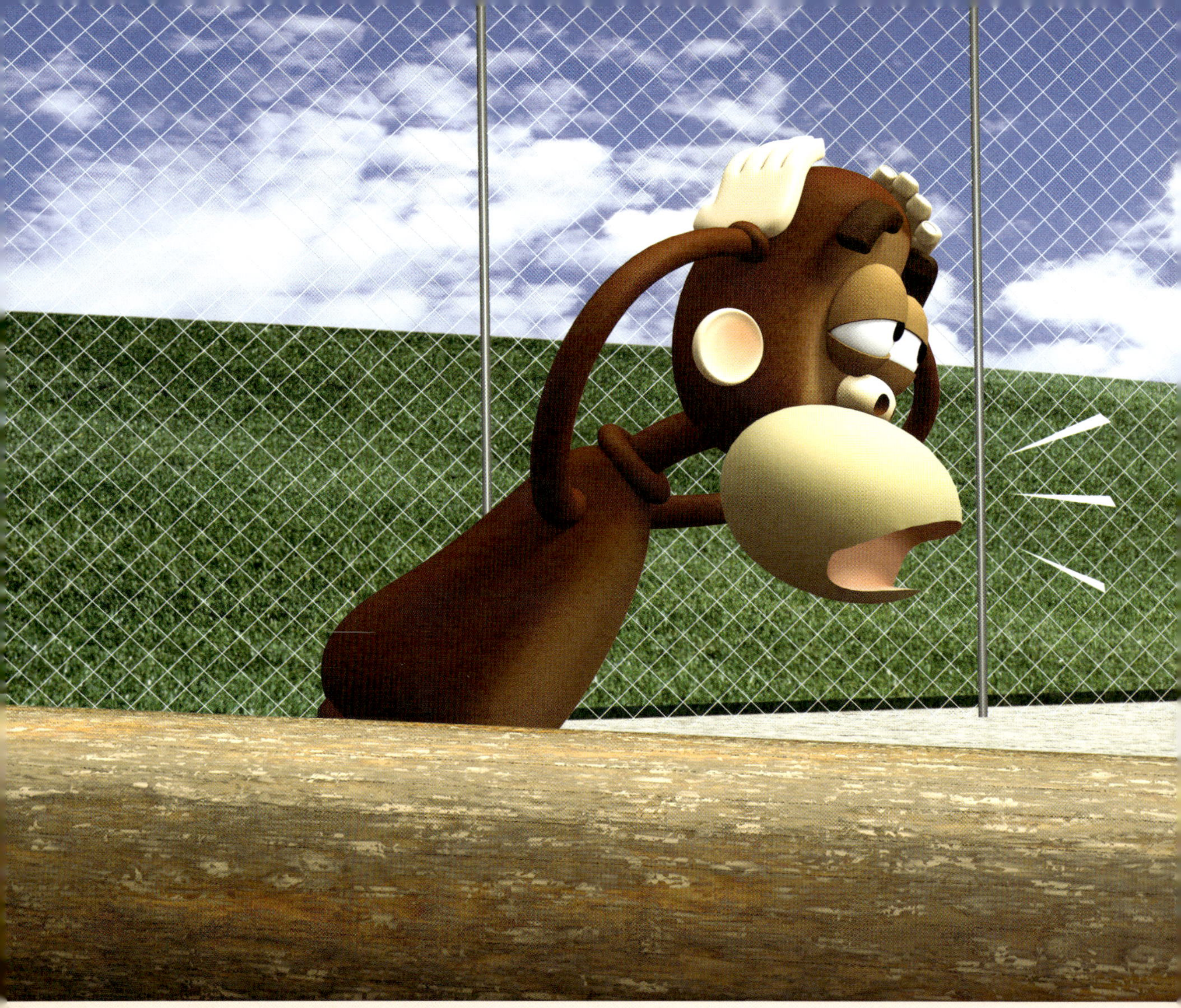

Dad is mad.

“It is a din!”

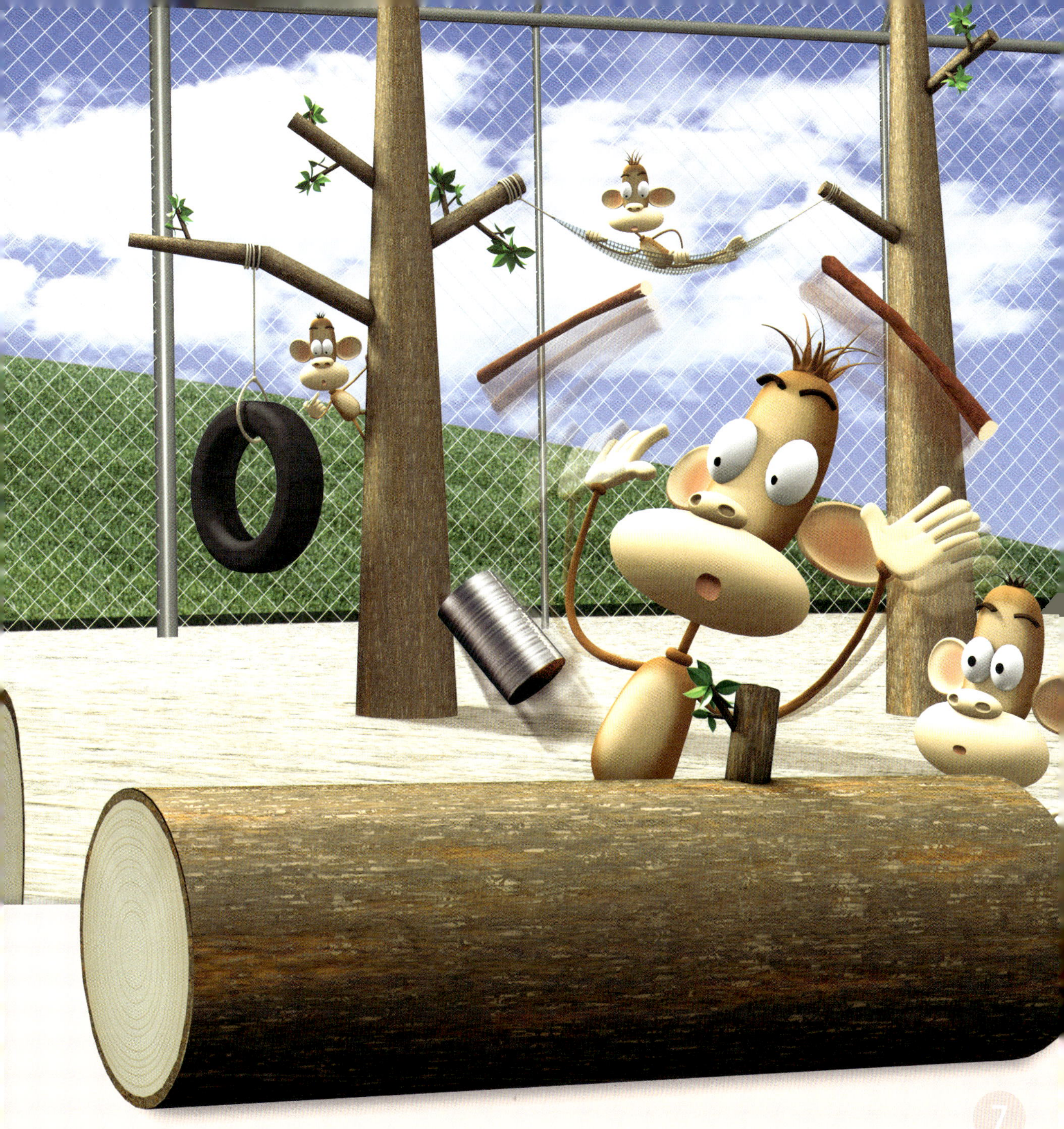

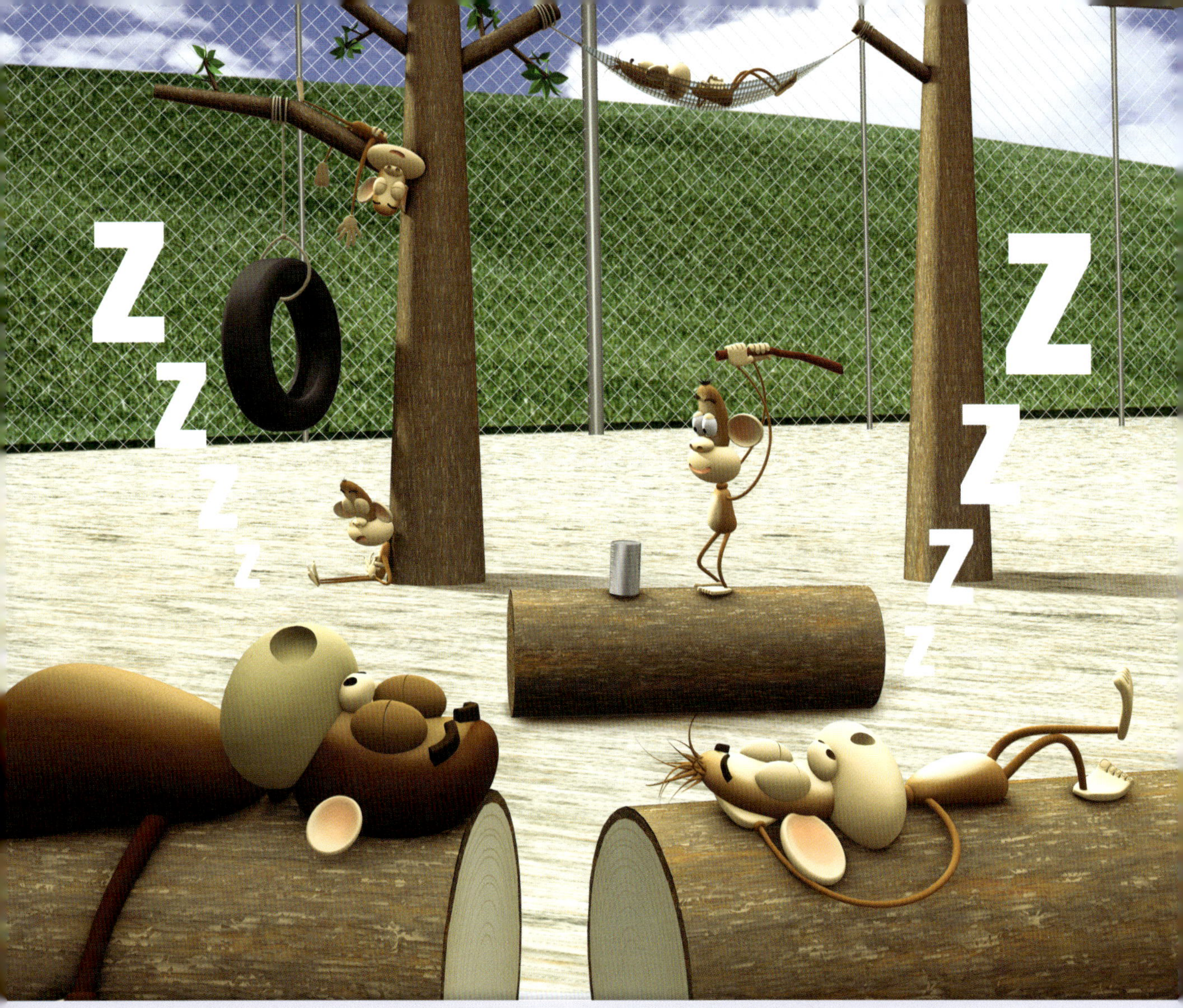

Dad naps. Tim naps.
Sam taps.